What If EVERYBODY Thought That?

Words by **Ellen Javernick**

Pictures by **Colleen Madden**

two lions

Published by Two Lions, New York
www.apub.com

Amazon, the Amazon logo, and Two Lions are trademarks of Amazon.com, Inc., or its affiliates.

ISBN-13: 9781542091374 (hardcover)
ISBN-10: 1542091373 (hardcover)

The illustrations are rendered in mixed media.
Book design by AndWorld Design

Printed in China
First Edition
10 9 8 7 6 5 4 3 2 1

maybe she's **SHY**. we should ask her to play with us.

I don't think she likes us.

To my brother, Peter, who proved everybody
wrong when they thought he'd never walk again.
—E. J.

Let's ride
back home
and make
COOKIES!

CLIP-CLOP!
CLIP-CLOP!

YAY,
COOKIES!

To Ms. S. and her SPARTANS—best day ever! XO
—C. M.

They might be wrong.

They might be wrong.

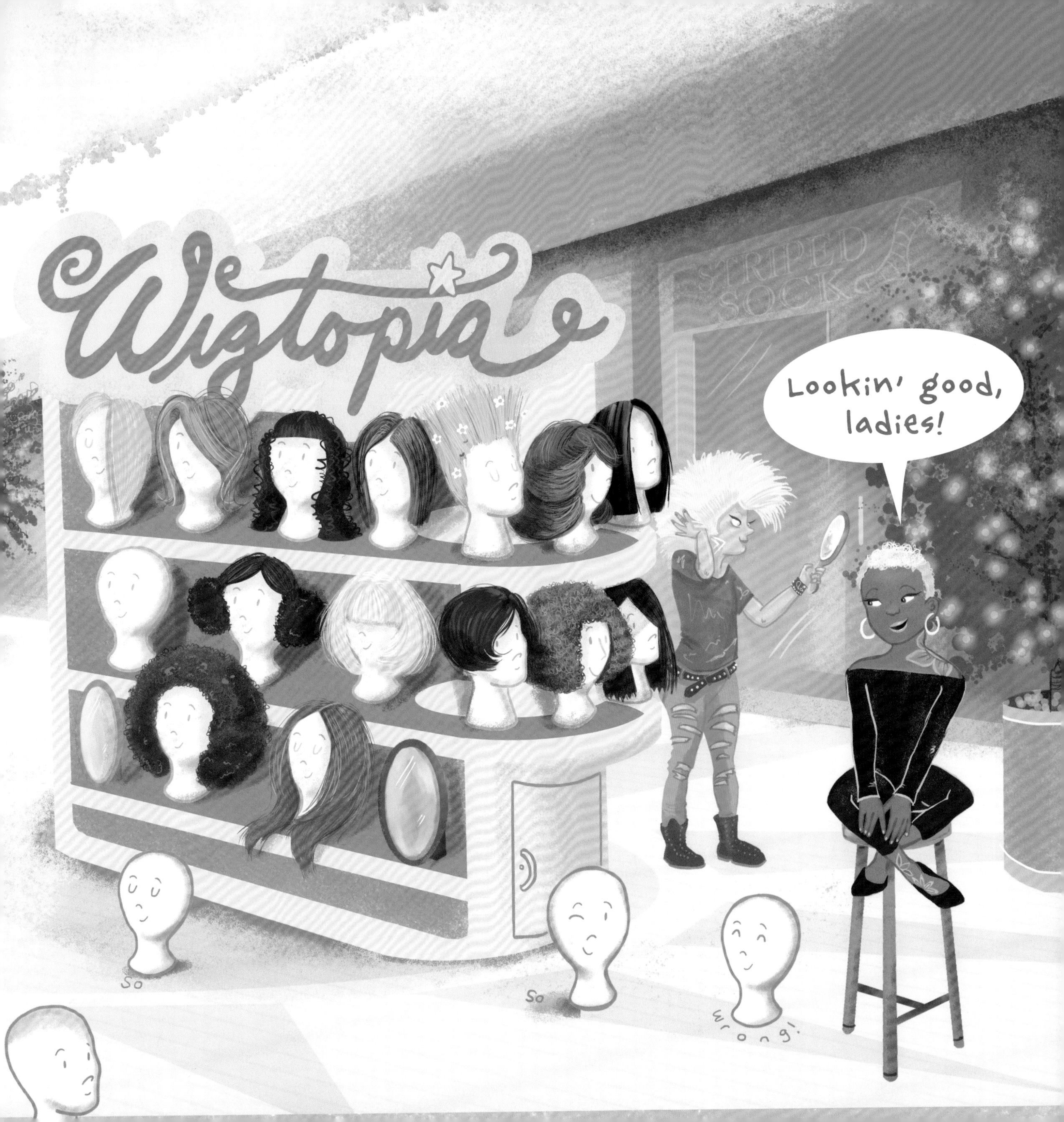
Wigtopia
STRIPED SOCK
Lookin' good, ladies!
So
So
wrong!

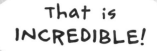

THEY...MIGHT...BE...WRONG!

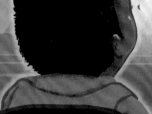

EVERYBODY SHOULD.